Make A Wish

Flairs and Glairs

Publication House

$\mathscr{D}$isclaimer

This is a work of fiction and solely represent the thoughts of the corresponding authors of the articles.
Our editors have tried their best to edit the content of all the authors and check the plagiarism.
All the write-ups in this book are unique and are only published in this book.
In case any plagiarism or error is found, only the author is responsible alone, and not the publisher or the Compilers.

Cover Designing and Book Formatting
Shubham Shah

Acknowledgement

Dear Almighty, thank you for blessing me with the power and zeal to be able to complete this Anthology. Also, Thank You dear parents, for trusting in me, and letting me work whenever I wanted. My family is the one who supported me for what I am today.

When it comes to this Anthology, I would like to start with Thanking the Co-authors, without your help and support, I would have never been able to complete it.

Thank You all of you, for being there. Much Love to all of You. I am glad to see you all standing by me.

Co Authors

1. Shubham Shah (Founder And Compiler)
2. Ishani Agarwal (Co Founder)
3. Ishika Agarwal
4. R.Karthikeyan
5. Dhivyadharshini. K
6. Sarumati Balagurunathan
7. Suganya
8. G.Anitha
9. Tamilelakkiya.S
10. S.Thirunirai Selvi
11. Nithyasri Gayatri
12. DHARANI.K
13. Kanaka Kumar
14. Saba Khan
15. Prasanna Devi K
16. B.Durga
17. R.Sumathi
18. A.Priyadharshini

Shubham Shah

(Founder- Flairs and Glairs)

Shubham Shah, entrepreneur at "Flairs & Glairs" a brand with dynamics in events organizing and cultural educational pan INDIA, He is a 26yr. old guy who recently has entered, the digital platform of imprinting emotions. He has initiated with his own open mic platform to help budding poets and aspiring writers under his brand named as "Teekhe Zasbaaat"

He is a commerce graduate from Bhagalpur City of Bihar.

He says Writing has impersonated him since childhood and he has now been writing for over a decade!

Cooking, on the other hand, is his passion! He also mentions, trying out new things just tickles him!

When asked sir, Why SPICY EMOTIONS?

He smiled and added, "agar jasbaat teekhe na ho toh wo jasbaat kaha" Spices are all that blends! So do his words!

As a chef, he presents to you his dish! Hot and freshly served! Taste it! Feel it! Enjoy it! You can also find his writing in the Solo book "Teekhe Zasbaaat" and 70+ anthologies. With his passion to explore opportunities across Platforms he is working with keen devotion and We wish him all the very best for his future ventures

Share your reviews on his

INSTAGRAM

    @spicy_emotions

    @shubham4shah

Or via email on

    shubham2shah@gmail.com

To stay tuned to his work and opportunities follow his business Handles

INSTAGRAM   FACEBOOK   YOUTUBE

    @flairsandglairs

    @teekhezasbaaat

WEBSITE:

    https://flairsandglairs.in/

    https://flairsandglairs.com/

Chingari ko apni dhadakta shola bana...

Rakh me bhi dabi aukat dikha...

Jungal hai tera... Apni dahaad suna...

Cheekh kar gae jo tujh par unhe... Apni sultanat se wakif karwa...

Samet le lapton me apni... Aur bhasm kar unke ahem ko...

Rehem ka raasta apna...

Par insaaniyat ko itna bhi na dafna ki rakh kar tere kandhe par pair wo apni hekdi dikhae...

Ishani Agarwal

(Co Founder- Flairs and Glairs)

Ishani Agarwal

Born and brought up in Kolkata, she has done her schooling and college from here itself. She is doing her post-graduation at the moment. Ishani loves talking to people around, and is excited for this new beginning of hers! Been a Compiler for 35+ Anthologies, and in the process for more, also, co-authored in 100+ Anthologies, Ishani is very Happy with how her life is turning out now!

Insta handle: Ishani_agarwal_quotes

Talking To You..

There is something about talking to you..
That makes me smile..
With you not there..
The smile from my face vanishes..
Your voice gives me the peace and solace that i was looking
for since so long..
Your messages make me blush most of the time..
It is with you, that I have the best time of my day..
Without you, life is incomplete..

Ishika Agarwal

Ishika is a 16 years old girl.

Writing for her is nothing else but a passion. She hails from the city of Joy and Art. She has been a Co-author in 30+ anthologies in the recent past, all adding on experiences to her. Been a part of India book of Record projects like Black and World Record projects like 15 wonders of Poetry, Ishika is paving her way to success.

I might not tell you this.
I might not send you this note ever but I need to get it out of my mind, my heart and my system.
So here it goes,
I have had enough.
I can't keep it inside me anymore.
I wanted to tell you something.
You were my childhood crush.
You were my teen crush and now you are my adult crush.
I have and always will love you.
But the problem is you don't love me and that eats me up everyday.
I want to be your life partner.
I want to be your partners in crime.
I love you.
I just wish you could be mine forever.

R.karthikeyan

He is karthikeyan, hailing from TAMILNADU. He loves writings , songs and the good vibes around him. He does mimicry and makes funover his circle . He loves cinema . He loves creativity. He wants to become a Director. He believes that he will shine one day .

Dark Beam

It was a chill afternoon . Sky was fresh after a rain . A girl of sixteen with a positive vibe was at a terrace , starring at a plaintain breezy dance . Every trees , colours , even the plain road on the day tried to say something to her . Her heart felt like a tulip in a world of cactus . A phonecall interrupted her with a random default ringtone . Not even without gazing over the screen , bangedoff the powerbutton . She just wanted to bludegeon with the surrounding . Fareaway , a blur beam of light arrested her vision over it and got her back to salad days . Those were the blossom days for her . A mellifluous combination of songs consoled her . The days where she was the only queen of her paradise . The ring of a church bell , frightened . The present still of night received her. She looked the sky as that she had never seen before . She got the memories of her grandma's words , that she do a cute ping to amaze her to narrates the short stories about the shooting star to spoonfeed her. Now, she searched all around the sky for a shooting star . She wanted to make a wish over a shooting star and get something too valuable and luxurious . But there was nothing for a sign of shooting star , except orb of night and the uncountables . Somewhat the manoeuvring of bats made her scare with vampire myths . She went back from the terrace with a longing heart for a shooting star . When she stepped into the living room , grand lighting fixtures and the floor of granites welcomed her warmly except her mom . Ever that she will never be there to do her stuffs . The voice over the TV with an unpleasant background score annoyed her . She just wanted to turn it off . When she came nearer to TV , there she saw a disastrous scene that her dad was struggling to breathe . She took him on her shoulders and ransacked to car. To make a call over for her family doctor, she turned on her phone . There she saw a lot of lost calls . She came to realize something with tears . As soon as her dad's tongue became abnormal in a colour combination of blue and violet . She screamed a lot infront of her family doctors house . Only the loudest decibel of silence became the reply . Suffocation of her father turned high and became unconscious . The scene was frozen with a silent emotional lachrymose breakout in the empty street . Suddenly an auto came with a jazzling horn , that usually south Indian auto's sounds . Auto driver gave a positive gesture to help them . Usually she had no more faith in religious words that " god never leaves the good hands " . Now the auto driver seemed to her like a god but as a little bit drunken creater. As soon as they arrived to a small street with congested buildings, there the people do sleep in that street even nearby stinky ditches. But the place seemed to be more familiar in her life . She experienced the moment as like a " Dejavu " . There was a small hospital with the fluctuations of lights on the welcome board display . Soon his father was taken by stretches into the hospital . A Doctor hurried to her in a nightdress and with a mask . She gave all the positive words that she can and left her saying that there is nothing to be worried and it's just a wheezing turned too worse because of irregular medication . The eyes of the doctor was more relevant to her as she sees regularly in photo . But , she can't get it right in that situation . Doctor called over the nurses there and asked to take her seat . They served her with a humble hospitality that they can do offer the most . She made a painful walk over the street . On being to the corner of the street , " HOW GIFTED , AM I ? " said herself . She looked into the sky and asked with a disgust feeling , "WHY HAVE U MADE US WITH UNEQUITY?" . As she believed , there will be some response . The response came like a star scratching over the sky with a speed of beam . Yeah, now she can't make everything better around her, by herself own . But, Her wish can . Now she wishes for the equity among the society . All like a flash , after years the city was well developed and she looked after her dad by withstanding on a own job . It will be nice to hear it as comics . In reality, there was no more changes in the city except her . She changed a lot and got unwrapped out of a common human's greediness . She turned into a writer of fantasies that lies slightly green with reality . She looked forward to help the needy out by her publishments . Every major press channels awaited for her callsheet even for a few minutes paid interview . The photoghraphers followed with the flashes around her beyond the red carpets . All of sudden she felt like she was slipping out on the stairs and woke up from her nightmare with an yellow ending . Because of sweating and little bit of suffocation , she opened the windows nearby making the way to gaze into the congested street that she is being inn , in her shack . She took a lantern hanging slight above in her own south Indian culture built rondavel and walked into the street for the shooting star to get the same dream with the same endings to be happened without those things that made her bawl.

Dhivyadharshini. K

"I am from Tamil Nadu.
I have a strong desire on writing and I love too pen the poem
which makes the readers to have view over in their inner mind.

Shooting Star

What is human body? Asked to her zeal granddaughter. Chai turned with her long black graceful hair along with her glowing skin and blushing cheeks. Her dazzling eyes started blinking by noticing granny's question. Through her soft and pinkish lips she smiled and replied it is a combination of nerves, heart, brain, lungs alike this universe has stealthy knots. Beyond the universe there are galaxy, Milky Way, Virgo super Clusters, Stars, dust clouds and other planets which is apart from the human mind. To the arid face woman the remembrance of the universe makes her astonishing always. The universe use to seduce her from the dwindle age. Therefore she want to fly over in the space. But it was frustrated and the mind devasted by futile. Now she wants her distinctive to reach the dignity. Perhaps, represent Chai to fly over the space who has proportionate qualities from bijou age. Besides, opened the first knot about shooting star and appended that Ancient Greek it is believed as a message of hope and to pull her years she attest the quotes of **Nicholas Sparks**

Summer romances end for all kinds of reasons. But when all is said and done, they have one thing in common: they are shooting stars – a spectacular moment of light in the heavens, a fleeting glimpse of eternity. And in a flash, they're gone. **[The Notebook]**

And assured with the saying of Bible Verses:

"Ah Lord God! Behold, Thou hast made the heaven and the earth by thy great power…There is nothing too hard for thee" Jeremiah [32:17]

Chai throw out the probe to Granny, from where the shooting star exists and asked her to describe it. Granny started elucidating her quest. The shooting stars are small asteroids and meteorites it starts burning in atmosphere when they collide with planet. Also, the shooting star is a symbol of Independence, Solitude and self – determining. The shooting star represents which gives changes in our life and in other side it stands for bad omens also Native American tribes believes it is a war omen, travelling spirits of Shamans and Heroes. Chai heart started gnawing to see the shooting star. She put off were it can be seen. In hushfull voice granny countered it is visible in the open sky. Everyday million of shooting star exists in this world to glimpse them there must be enough patience. After hours they moved from river bank to get forty winks. Chai saw a gleaming light from sky and became jubilant that it was serendipity. It moves as a double leopard within a second and Chai attained a bizarre and sublime feeling together. Suddenly remained her Granny saying by seeing a shooting star, our wishes come true. To the next she confused what does the shooting star brought now a good fortune or a bad omen. Therefore by closing her eyes with sharp eyelids wished that world must be filled with the fragrance of love and smile to the peace must be scattered. Abruptly she woke up from sleep and groaned about the dream. Chai started envisage of shooting star through pleasing eye.

Shooting Star

It was tranquil,
The world was discolored,
My mind became despondent,
I went into the gloomy and somber night,
With the melancholy heart,
I decent the red blood,
A sudden dazzle is originated,
My eyes struck with the spark,
The meteor moves as rabbit,
My mind deliberate the lexical of legend,
By glimpsing the shooting star,
Our inclination will betide,
As it wriggle in jiffy;
Besides our glum desist.

Sarumati Balagurunathan

"She is Sarumati Balagurunathan from Karur.
She loves nature and believes in filial love.Her soulmate is music. She thinks Nothing as prior than her mother's happiness".

A Regained Hope

It was almost the mighty dark room. She can no more keep her eyes closed. Opening the window by relaxing the curtains, she saw the moon with its height of peacefulness. She thought whether she was called by the moon to contract the distance. Losing down the hair band and Keeping her arms folded within one into another. She came out to the balcony with her arms accompany. Chuckling herself. She gone through with her memories back.

The man sleeping in the bed, woke up by realizing that she wasn't nearby. Murmuring Sithru..!! Sithuru..!!!

Even more rather than searching his girl his first and foremost priority goes to his spectacles. Anyhow finding and grabbing it he somehow manages to find her standing in the balcony as being the biggest competitor to the moon. Her feathery hairs waves as if the ocean does. Something in her makes his lip to get closed and move nearby in Silence. The girl feels him

behind and turns towards him. No more words just an eye

contact.

' Hey ! Why do you want me to get confused in the count of moon?'he asks with a lovely smile.

She in blush has no words in reply. Again she starts within an enthusiastic voice,

Lucer, 'Is the Shooting star yet to come.?'

He as if yawning herself inside the mouth, 'What.? Shooting star uh.?'

'Yep! Shooting star! When it arrives we can make a wish to come true.

What is this Sithara? Do you want me to believe it in.? Okay! I believe so. Please do come it's already twenty- five to two. Getting somewhat outraged, she begins to stand there stubborn, not even an inch to be moved with him.

She herself is a child, now she is a mother to a child. Thinking it for a minute Kavish stood nearby holding her hands. Their pampered chat started over there. He asks about the Shooting star again.

She started by saying. ' one day during my 21st birthday I came to know about the Shooting star through my Granny. She said to make a wish when it passes. On the strange night waiting for the Shooting star everyone was busy in selecting their wish. I too was confused whether to ask Browine or diary milk. But when the Shooting star crossed on the sky, everybody looking at it and closed their eyes by praying something. But I was the only one who got very much confused with wide opened eye an lovely figure stretched out in front of the star in the terrace. With an wide opened eye and mouth I just stared at him. only thing sprang into my mind was

he, Why shouldn't I meet him again.? That lovely smile, Sharp eyes, folded shirt, elegant walk. He was almost like the shooting star.

Interrupting her gracious speech, with a ridicule laugh, 'Did you see him again? Sithuru',he asked.

The moment he asked she said, ' No he was the one whom I was putting on my head on his shoulder now'. With trauma, he turned to her. She with her full confidence, said that shooting star was the only reason behind their wedlock.

Being a space Engineer , Kavish was not propounded with the words of her. But somehow managed to make her repose.

The very next day, Sithara was excited about the Shooting star. Kavish getting irritated not showing off the face somehow managed to get ready for his work.

Sending off him, Sithara started her daily routine. Kavish not even stepped into his work site received a call which interrupted his wish towards his colleague. His pink face turned into red, he sprint as if to get into something. As his bike started it at last reached the hospital.

Running to the reception, he said 'Sithara .... pregnancy case'. She replied 'Emergency ward.. Not even she completed the sentence but then he reached the ward..'

He went nearby her, She almost started blabbering, pinching, punching, and even pulling his hair. He was unbearable to her pain. Nothing can be done. Almost his tears busted out. It is almost 2 hours now but still the baby couldn't peel out. Helplessly, he went near the statue of God in the hospital. There he kneeled down and started blabbering like anything. Her pains became his tears. He felt like dying for something wrong. Mindful of questions . Almost he was the fainted up.! No friends or the relatives could make him up.

And now roaming like a gypsy he went along the crowd, not even having any idea where they were moving to. He as the herd went to see what is happening through the window.

Everyone seeing the Shooting star prayed out something. He not even knowing him started to pray for his lovable kitty! Sithara..!!

When he opened out his eyes he heard a bud crying sound....!!!!!

Really dunno is this because of the wish he made..!!
But her love made him to believe it so..!!!

Suganya

I'm Suganya from Tamilnadu. I'm an engineer who like to explore in many ways. I always try to improve my passions like story writing and poem writing in Tamil and English. And so my passions become my hobbies. Everyday I'm looking forward to grab opportunities to learn more and more

My Mom - A Shooting Star

A girl who undergoes schooling used to watch the stars in the sky every night and dreams about her future.

At night, after having dinner she took her belongings to sleep in the terrace.

""Wish!.....I wish ...? To be a doctor or an engineer? No... no... I wish to be a baby girl for my mom. Yes,of course... I'm the baby girl...and my mom is an angel...""

""A queen who rules the heart of her children. Still I couldn't able to find how she could able to love after all a flesh and bone and care for it. She sacrificed her whole life for us. She doesn't felt for giving up everything ,except her self-respect and courage in front of others, because for her children. She never regretted her children wish.""

""Never and ever!!""

""But why? ""

""She might realised that she could be the future of her children. Why doesn't she care about her future and her dreams?""

""Why does she put it off?""

""What makes her to do this?""

""How is it possible?""

""Oh God!!!""

""Why don't I think in a different perception? She don't even tell us about her dreams? If asked she would say ""You are my dream"" . Then what it would be during her childhood?""

""I should know about that? But how? I should get an idea? Quick...quick..."" I threatened my mind.

"" If I ask to her directly, she would definitely ignore me. Then, ??? Yeah.. got it...""

(After finding her school diary)

The diary was almost devastated. They are ruled pages and many of them seem to be empty and spoiled.(Those pages describes her empty heart and spoiled dream)

(After viewing almost half of the diary)

Oh god..I think I should find some other way. There is no trace of what I wish to see.""

 At last, there is a page left with royal blue ink dotted as letters.

"" Yes... I hope this could be the one I'm looking for!"" With full of excitement and the happiest feel that comes when our team gets victory in India Vs Pakistan cricket match, with the same enthusiasm I looked it forward ,

The letters in the line obviously describes the clarity of her dream. Read in a husky voice and checked whether anybody coming nearby.

Then I started to read the first line "" If I were a doctor...""

Those words are not just letters, but passion and dedication.

(That night with the melted heart,I started to watch the stars,it looked even prettier and dazzling... It seem to be holding dreams(achieved) of many moms hanging just like that and suddenly a shooting star appeared...

""What those shooting stars mean?""

Though my mind processed fast, I couldn't get the answer. But my heart said ""Those shooting stars are the dreams of the moms that they sacrificed and so it is not hanging in the sky to fill the dark with shine.""

""They are meant to fill the dreams of her children by her sacrifice""

("""Shooting stars...a lot of shooting stars...oh..oh!!?.. it's a meteor stream""" a voice screaming)

Suddenly looking at the sky,

But this time, I changed my wish. ""Oh! Meteor stream!! Oh! Meteor stream!! I hope you would make all my wishes true...., I wish that's my mom's dream should come true.""

 Still many moms are like shooting stars

falling from the sky

for her children to fly....

G.Anitha

She Loves Writing Books And Interested In The Field Of Teaching.She Considers Her Parents Happiness As The Biggest Thing In The World

Make A Wish

It was a pleasant night in one winter. Akila a good looking and courageous lady. She had completed her P.HD   and working as a linguistic researcher.

She used to spend her night by counting stars and enjoying the view of moon. She would also wait for shooting star to make her wish.

On that night, she was preparing the document for her research and it was to complete. She was hearing the voice of her mother calling her to take her supper.

It was around 10.30 P.M , after completion of her work , she moved to take supper .She was enduring to tare the chappathi which was hard because it was prepared before three hours. After completion of her dinner , she moved to upstairs of her house to enjoy the galaxies and to make her wish.

The fresh air made her to calm her mind and reminiscence the pleasant incidents which happened in her life . The trees swayed and the sounds of the birds in the nest gave soothing to her ears and gave piece of mind.

She stared at the sky to find out the meteor stream and shooting star to make her wish as usual. Her was only one from her childhood.

Akila was at the age of 12 after completing her home work she went to bed. That was one midnight in winter season and there was heavy rainfall.It was so chill and cold. She felt shivering and covered her all over body using blanket.

It was around 12 o' clock in midnight. She was disturbed by the voice of mumbling. Due to continuous sound mumbling and murmuring she awakened from the bed without disturbing her mother.

She had looked the way of sound which disturbed her sleep. She had seen the   about ten children who were sleeping without blankets or even without any pillows .They were seemed to marginal and street children . Most of them were seemed to be parentless.

Some children were shivering and mumbling in that snowfall night. In other side some of them were starving without having sense of cold. Their eyes were tried and bodies were almost in miserable condition.

She had thought the different lifestyle of children in the world which was provided by the God .This made her to realize the value of parents ,food and education .

She went out from her main door of her house to see the children. The condition of children intended to do something to them in her life.

She provided blankets and chappathies to children. she had seen the gratitude behind their eye and smile.

From that day , she had been helping them by providing education in evening and in weekends. She was providing basic amenities to them in her earnings. This had been giving satisification and heart fulfillment to her .

Smile of children gave her more cheerful and considered as silhouette of God.

On that day onwards, she had been wishing only one thing while seeing shooting stars everyday that was to get   all amenities to marginalized and   street children in the world . They should get love and support in some form of ways.

This had been her wish everyday to shooting star.

Humanity is more essential to human being we can prove that only in the way of spreading love and being to support to miserables.   .It's a silhouette of God .Helping to needy and poor children make us satification. we can feel only by doing it.

Tamilelakkiya.S

She is Tamilelakkiya hailing from Tamilnadu. She Loves to narrate and hear stories . And she writes qoutes during her leisure .Her biggest aim is to become a Director .Many criticized her for this aim,but she wants to prove herself before them

Eros

Men and women are seprated by two categories. One ,a pure friendship and other , love.The word love reflects pure soul. And it gives most beautiful feel and sometimes soreness too. And her comes the character Elakkiyan and Harsini .They were childhood besties. As day passes, they grown up and they were in 9th std.And this was the time which made elakkiyan to fell in love with harsini.He doesn't know how to express his love towards to

 Harsini, he was so embraced to express his love towards her. And one day he decide to convey his love to her and the words he quoted in text is,

his love to her and the words is, ""WILL YOU MARRY ME HARSINI?"" ,and after seeing

 this ,she gone blank, doesn't,

 know what to do further. And after that ,they were seprated solidly for 6 months.After that long gap , both met under a tree where they usually meet.

 Harsini stood nerves , and

elakkiyan came there by and said that he was eager to know the reply from her,so he went asking again,"" I'm excited to know the word I expect from you"",So please tell me your's opinion.But ,she didn't reply anything,she felt happy but deep something made her frightened and but suddenly,

she looked at his eyes and said nothing. And on seeing her eyes,he understood her love

she felt love for him.

And they both were, very happy and they looked like made for each other.

Elakkiyan usually tells her that, "" The thing I expect from

you is, I need you by my side always and I promising you that
I will be there for you no matter
 what"".
Both cared each other and loved each other a lot ,they seem to
be a cute couples.
 One day they went to a jaunt ,and that place was so
 cool and awesome ,it was dam named , "" Aliyar"", which
was a good placed to visit. And there,Harsini and elakiyan
 both looked their eyes and
and their heart started to melt,
both walked on that side by holding their hands ,and again
 they made a promise to each other and they shared their love.
Suddenly, elakiyan parents who came by that side noticed it
and beaten him hard and took him from that place.Their
parents seprated elakiyan and harsini . But,on other side
Harsini was longing for him . She didnt even receive any
mesages, phone calls, letters from him. She couldn't find a
single way to contact him.
Elakiyan by his parents compulsion, went to abroad but
harsini was not informed about that.Both broken a lot. Harsini
Kept on thinking about him
 everyday , and whether they will get married or not.But ,she
believed very strongly that he
Will come.

Usually, Harsini relaxes herself by reading books.One day
while she was reading a book ,she came to know about
shooting star. It was so interesting and she read further and
noticed a sentences that," If two shooting comes together and

if one see it sure that person will be married to the one, she(or) he loves truely"'

Luckily after reading this elakkiyan contacted her and said that he returned from abroad and he planned for a meet.Then, she said about the
 shooting star's prophecy to him .And one next day in their meet, they travelled many places in search of the shooting star.And finally they both sawn it, in the same aliyar dam where they was caught by elakian parents.
The very next day elakkiyan came with his parents and they agreed to marry elakiyan to harsini.
Elakkiyan presented a ring
and said Harsini that,""I will never
leave you"",suddenly Harsini blinked her eyes and she got amazed on seeing the two shooting again and it reflected their face.

And it was exactly 3 AM ,both stood in terrace and looked the sky for the farce of shooting
 star and spelled together that,
""I will be always there for you no matter what "".
And they thanked the shooting star for making their "dream into real ,and got married and lived happily"

S.Thirunirai Selvi

36

She is ThiruniraiSelvi, from Tamilnadu. She is a teacher .She loves music and craft works. She loves to read books and loves to write .She loves to improve herself from the errors and Believes in hardwork

A Wait

Life we live are the greatest gift we had, have and will have. Life always gives one thing back at its each count that is memories. And to say now, I have only the beautiful memories I got from my life, which is captured like beautiful scenery in my sight, and unmatchable happiness in my words and unbreakable love in my heart. Everything seems like happened yesterday, but now I'm far apart from that beautiful life that turned into memories. It's an everlasting journey, where I and my cute family crossed. It's a small house, but for me it's a palace where my dad and mom are the king and queen, and I'm the only princess over there. Years rolled, I got three sisters and a little brother and I'm the eldest of all, not only in age but also from beatings that I get from my mom ,and to say about my father he is also strict but I'm his favorite. And my grandmother too stayed with us, to say about her, she is a strong lady, great hard worker and a sweetest person I had ever seen, whenever we scare at something she is the one who hugs us tight and escapes us from those fears. Still, I can remember that day exactly; it was a full moon night where everyone sat outside in our terrace to have dinner .Usually our grandmother tells us lot of stories at bed time, and during this scene she said us the story of galaxy and also more about the stars that twinkling up in that beautiful sky. She went on saying about them .Suddenly, I felt something in the sky, I couldn't see it clearly but partially it seemed like a star, it started to raise me question within myself."Do stars run? If not so then how it fell from that place? This question of mine confused me, so I broke my confusion to granny .This question of mine made her to laugh then she took me on his lap, hugged me warmly and said that it was a shooting star. It was appointed by our almighty to help those in need. So, it watches every little one down the earth, examines them and when it notifies a true soul it fades down turning as a wish to them. After explaining she looked at my face and said, "My little girl had become a favorite soul to the shooting star, that's why the fall of the shooting star fallen on your sight, now make a wish in your heart my dear", she asked me to close my eyes and ask for wish, I did as she said. And suddenly, a sound frightened me and I woke up, and then I found myself in a orphanage, Yeah! I lost my family in a festival and now I'm far apart not alone from the memories but also from my family. I miss my cute family , I wish to hear the scolding's of my mom and dad and heart melts for my grannies hug and my hands are searching to hold my little brother and sisters. Those memories makes me live here. Then I gone near the window and stared at the sky, tears started to shed, my eyes searched for shooting star again, wishing show me the place of my family. Everyday my day ends with a hope to see the shooting star and every morning it starts with a wish to be in my home with the carvings of my family love.

Tears in heart shatter the agony day and night
Searching for shooting star in sleepless fright
Wishing to show the lovable place of my past
Waiting to backup the treasured memory I lost

Nithyasri Gayatri

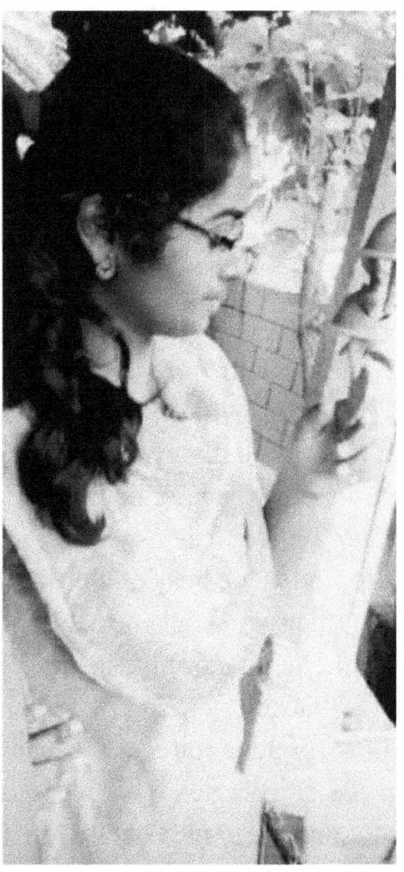

She is Nithyasri a college student from Dharapuram a town in Tamil Nadu.She is interested in reading horror stories.She came forward to express her best in writing.Hope this will make her to lead for the next step of her journey.

Fall For A Curse

MIC is my name; I'm already eighteen and a graduate. In life, one thing that drives me crazy is Adventure, yeah! I love adventure, especially with my friends. And this time we planned to visit the hills near by our city. Our trip started next day and we are half of the way to hills. Finally, we reached the hills after trucking for 5 hours. The sun gone to its bed and it was dark than normal, we couldn't find a moon and stars over there .It was totally strange to us, and we at a distance something resembled like light, to examine it we stepped forward towards and found a village there. We went inside the village and stayed there for that night. The villagers there gave us food and they behaved with us in a friendly manner, we introduced our self and said about our trucking there in hills. An old man from the crowd came forward and warned us not to go visit the center of the forest, especially not to go near the big tree which is fenced .One hearing this my friends mocked them for saying so ,then we thanked them and left the place. After reaching the shelter one of my friends went on speaking about the big tree till morning. Next day we started our search in the forest seeking for adventure and reached the big tree at the center which was surrounded by fence made up of thorns, we took a shot of it and we came back to the shelter by night. And he again started to spell about the tree, he said that, "there must be some treasures below the tree and that's why the old man is blocking ours way to it and now I'm going to find the way to deserve it". I restricted his way, but he didn't hear my words. He moved towards the tree along with tools to dig and in order to engulf him ,the tree made a trick to increase his curiosity by giving a shiny material under the fence .By finding the shiny material, he came back to the shelter to show us that these things are just to stop our way from taking the treasure and he asked us to come along with him. I ignored him and went inside the shelter, but other two friends went along with him. Minutes gone, and I felt bored and went on seeing the snaps that we took today and my fear started to rise when I looked at the picture that we took along with the big tree, I found that place of tree empty, then I rushed to my friends but when I reached that place, I found no one there except the tree, but somewhere I could hear my friends seeking for help .Then went back to the village to seek some help, When I rushed to the people, they said me about the curse they got because of a dead and he is the one who stays within the tree and he increase his power by engulfing them , to take them back one should close the bed of dead that paves the way of light and when the twinkle fells .Then I rushed towards the graveyard ,the bed of dead with lots of troubles and illusions in between and closed it . At once the moon and stars appeared, which is light source and   waited for the fall of star to make my wish for to destroy the dead and tree by saving my friends life .At a blink the shooting star appeared, and I made my wish and brought back my friends and few people within the tree Finally, the dead gone back to its bed, and tree covered with blossoms. And we moved to our shelter to pack up. And this trip made my life the most adventurous one.

We left the place with memories behind

Dharani.K

"She is Dharanikrish A selenophile Fond of Moon .
She loves to travel ""A Walking wanderer"" Where she used
to make people comfortable with her speech always simply in
Love! She loves sandals That's her current favorite!! People
says she is Hard to have
Harder to have Impossible to forget!! She believes in
Love light Hope !

An Open Wish

With Hope, Love, Light

Hello, Hello, Hello!

Hey! Shooting Star.

I'm lucky enough to witness you the First time
This night is a dream come true ...
Is this a regular Night or a fairy Night? Can you tell?

Cheers to this Beautiful Night.
It's time to make a wish.!

Are you playing a peek-a -boo!!
Like stop, stop, stop!

My Eyes Are Twinkling and I got teary Eyes when I spot you,
so stop! For a minute. Wow I Mesmerized by your Beauty.

Okay!
Can't you take my wish peacefully
 Soon Thereafter!
Do you have any idea about how I Love making dream Home
of mine?
Yes......
The dream that I can't live without a day.
That big Desire is strong! And have been craving for the
Entire life.

Okay but I always want this Dream to be a Real one around me, It feels good when I have my ""Fancy become True""!!
I bet you one day you will see my beautiful mornings and Nights with all lovely guests and their warmest Welcome To My ""Fantasy ""With the Entrance arch to keep it all light and bright.
And my Fancy home will be simplicity with Ultimate sophistication!

 Big Grand Beautiful!!!

My Space:
There is something about color,
Yes!

So Decide to color with black white shade….
Just dropping the back drop with lights sparkling.
With Edges of soft Corner
 Will Make memories on the wall with serious settings that would stay for life!!
And
Curtains with Trendiness   In ""Too much black ""
Fashion on point!
And Top Notch
Will come up with a little cage for My Wagging Tail;
With a huge Happiness!
Isn't it?
Always wanted my dreamy to look as Fantasy as possible!
With love
Fairy in a Fairyland

This Is My Journey At The Moment

One night I was staring at the moon on the terrace. Then a comet appeared. It was not known what it was at first but only later it became known that it was a comet. It was like asking me a question about something. i am a disabled person. Yet that thought never occurred to me. But sometimes it made me realize my disability.

Because it seemed on that day that the action of time must come to the fore and the i must be born with no disability. Yes I have had many failures in my life due to this disability. I would have fulfilled my mother's wish if I had been born without disability alone.

The opportunity to go abroad was snatched away by my disability. I have had many failures in many places. I wondered what was the point of living well anymore. At that moment something powerful stopped me. It might even have been my dad. I made the life i live meaningful. so I joined as a good teacher.

i joined the teaching profession without slightest thought that the students would make fun of me. But as soon as i saw those students an unconditional affection ran through me.

From the day I joined this mission I threw away my disability. I also enjoyed the way the students their studies. My mother's wish was to become a good doctor. She wanted to give treatment to people like me for free.

I asked Will you remove my disability to the comet for a while and transform me into a new man? .
He is born as a new man without any disability as he thought. I fulfilled mother's wishes. my succeeded in everything my fails in life.

The period he asked for ends. Meets the comet again. he thanks to comet.

The comet asked now you are happy ? If I had been born without any disability I would have only fulfilled my mother's wish..The idea that I should achieve only because I was born with a disability seemed too much.I'm happier than that now.

But today I am a teacher fulfilling the desires of many students. I am making good students. I also share in the joy they achieve .
That said this event is enough to add pride to my mom. Hearing this the comet looked very surprised and greeted him and left.

Saba Khan

Saba khan was born in new Delhi. She completed her schooling from Aligarh muslim university, Aligarh. She is involved here in so many communities literature projects. She began writing poetry while a student at Subharti University, at which she made the decision to become both a poet and a doctor. She decided to be known by her pen name Ss Khan. Her work as a poet and story writer has been started with her poem " Wo Ek Khwab Tha"published in the magazine "Taare Zameen Par" In 2019. She is not just a good poet but a wonderful and lovely person. Regarding of the popular literary trends of the time, she writes the things are close to her heart.

एक छोटी से खुहाइश

तारों की चमकती हुई वो राते
बातों से भरी वो मुलाकाते
दिल मे छुपे हुए कुछ जज़्बात
आँखों मै केद वो नुरानी चेरा
खुशियों की भरी वो शाम
होंठ पे खिलखिलाती वो हसीं
काश वो शाम फिर से आ जाए
एक छोटी सी खुहाइश है
जो शायद पूरी हो जये
फिर से वो वक़्त साथ हो
फिर से वो राते साथ हो
तारों से बातें एक साथ करे
उस चाँद की चमक साथ देखे
काश वो शाम फिर से आ जाए
एक छोटी सी खुहाइश है
जो शयद पूरी हो जये.....

एक प्यारी सी दुआ

दुआ है उन चमकते सितारों से
दुआ है उस चाँद से
दुआ है उस नुरानी शाम से
के, फिर से आ जाए
वो बाते वो मुलाकाते
वो मीठी सी याद आई
फिर से अजय
कोई साथ हो न हो कोई फर्क नहीं
उस चाँद की नूरानीयत ही काफी है खुद की ख़ुशी के लिए
सुकून का एक जरिया उन सितारों से मिलकाते
ज़िन्दगी मे कितने ही गम क्यू न हो
रात होते ही वो ख़ुशी बन जाते थे
पता नही था हम इतने मसरूफ़ हो जायेगे
उस रात से मिलना ही भूल जयेगे
आज अकेले है वो राते याद आयी
दिल से फिर वही दुआ आयी
के, फिर से अजय वही सब
यही एक प्यारी से दुआ है....."

Prasanna Devi K

""Lock the soul in the Oyster of Arts
 Hang it in the Walls of Treasure
 To live beyond Generation!!!""
- LK Prasanna

Prasanna Devi, who goes by the pen name LK Prasanna, an optimistic writer who wishes to be ""Voice for Voiceless"". According to her, Poetry is like ""the Pearl of Joy, which is taken out of Nacre of Memory to Design the Ornament of beautiful Life"". She manifests the beauty of nature through her frame of poetry. She feels nature quenches her thirst in the search of gaiety in life.

Shadows

It hits me hard
I switch off the lights and get into my blankets
I try to rest my eyes in a deep sleep but I couldn't
Tears roll down to express the pain of secrets
I feel some hands start chasing me
I wish to run to the shelter of womb
The cry of pleads echoes in my ears
The stains of pain print in the walls of the buried truth

Huge cry for justice waits in the gate of courts
Truth wraps behind the bars of Injustice
Years run with pains of blame
Words roll out to question the framed crime
I wake up with the questions of Injustice
Sleepless night continues
Deepen with sorrows of secrets
I wish to be a Bolide for the hidden truth.

At The Roadside

Lights on!!!
Screeches ends!!
Puzzles bared.
Pinning Knight waits to meet his Lady Title
Gates of castle opens!!
Buzz bees rush out in search of honey.
Golden chariot waits for Her.

Mist comes down to announce her arrival
Like a lady tulip, she blooms out from the castle
With the wand, Knight freezes the Biffles
Silence surrounds them
Knight steps forward with the bouquet of Love
Eyes of knight say "" Tu Me Manques""
Spark of the falling star
 Breaks the magical moment.

Blossoms

He said, ""No Idea""
Chapter ends there
She closes the book and smiles
Time moves
She dreams about a dense Forest,
Where sound of quarrels wake her
She moves towards it and finds her own instincts
A warning of great destruction awaits her
Frightened eyes waits for the dawn
Drained legs walk to find mirth in it.
She hears the hooting of an owl nearby
She rests herself near a clustered cherry blossoms
She falls asleep to escape from the dusky night.
Dewdrops fall from the murky leaves and wake her up
A comet runs down the sky to enlighten the place of shady
Suddenly, he breaks the prison of crystal
And gives a rosa and says ""lo siento mucho""

B.Durga

She is Durga ... She is a Nature lover , Artist and She is extremely curious about Adventure and Photography... Her moto is "Train your mind to see good in every situation and to be positive always"

Samutra

After a hard adventure, I am returning back to my home. I feel weary. My eyes posture tiredness. Even though my eyes are wearied they are holding on to see the heavenliness of our village.

Our village is blessed with greenish sky-high trees, running river with shrubs on the one and the other shores. Trees are the home of non-identical varieties of Birds .My house is nested in the mid of coconut trees.

I am Samutra. I am hushed, meek, humble. I am dusky skinned, long haired girl with medium height. I am interested in cooking and curious about adventure. I am born in a traditional family. My father is an agriculturist and he has more hope on culture and society. My mother is a home maker. She is educated but not sent to job. I have an younger brother who is doing standard 9th. As I am the elder one I am given more responsibility and authority than my brother.

I have completed my schooling in Government school at my village and have scored good marks in my board examination. I am interested in Marine studies. So I have chosen B.SC Oceanography. I have to go out of my village for my higher studies. I am not aware of the outer world. Why because I am not sent out from my home. Only thing that I have known is my family and village. I am afraid to go out for studies. For the first time I am going out.

Finally I have joined Marine college at Kerala and stayed in hostel. It is really a hard time at hostel without my family. Time heals everything and even changes everything. Days have passed by thinking my family.

I have got three caring and believable friends. Each have a uniqueness in their characters. We have stayed at same hostel room . We all have a common interest in adventure. We all love adventure. My friends call me Sam. I feel very comfortable with that name.

Days have passed. We have stepped into our final year. We have got our final year project. So we have to go to ocean for our project research work. We people have thought it as an good adventure.

After a couple of days we have started our research work. We have found a boatman and have travelled in a boat with his help. Our tutor advices us not to go so interior into the ocean. But we have ignored that.

The sea seems to be silent and water waves look majestic. It have taken several hours for us to finish our research work. The day wanes the moon claims up. So we have decided to return. Suddenly a monster waves have stricken our boat. We have found a sudden collapse. Everyone starts fell into the water. We couldn't see any more. The sea water is as cool as ice. I have felt myself drowned inside the water. It is quite difficult for me to breathe. I have felt that my life had come to an end. As a spark for my new life, I have seen a Shooting Star. We have a faith in our village that Shooting Star is a symbol of virtue and goodness. I make a wish an seeing the star as everyone should return to shore safely. A new hope arise in my heart. I have a strong determination not to give up. I have gained my strength to swim. Fortunately I have found a broken part of the boat. It is much enough for me to sit. I move towards it and clasp it tightly. I am slim so that I can easily settle in that part.

Darkness prevails, skies are filled with stars, sea wave have changed into ordinary. Luckily I found a boat and called them for help. My voice seems so louder than before. The people in that boat have recognized the need of the hour and started to do first aid. I can't bear the chillness. We are saved by them. The incident of drowning into the sea was narrated to the people by us after the survival. We thank them. We successfully have submitted our project. Our college life have come to an end.

Conductor whistles. I have come back to reality. I can see the tall tree from the windows of the bus. After a prolonged travel. I have reached my home. My heart is filled with peacefulness and warmth. Every hard time teach us a new lesson. I have become more valiant person."

S.Sumathi

She is S.Sumathi living in Dharapuram.Working as a teacher and married to Ravindran also a teacher.She has loved stories which were described by her mother .She is blessed with two children are boys.She recalls her past life in this story.

Life of Mine

It's a morning, exactly 4 AM. My mobile waked me up with its irritating tone. I started to cough and searched for water and finally found the pitcher empty, it made me furious. The worst ever feeling is getting irritated at the start of a day, that last whole day making me stressed and it's a routine thing in my life.

And to refresh me I went to my balcony, whenever I feel stressed I move there, it makes me relaxed. In my balcony, I have a parrot named "shintu", she is 2 weeks old and she has a beautiful voice .And" Casper ", he is my kitty and he sleeps lethargically in the couch placed there and my beautiful rose plants which gives me perfumed smell, and those pleasant sound of birds chirping and the chillness filled breeze which hugs me over there and the pour of mirth by moon, these are enough to make me cool when I'm hyper tensed. Oh! Oops, I forgot to intro my "gulu gulu" my Aquarians, these two are the ever beautiful tailed fish, long and shiny blue colored .After refreshing me I moved to kitchen to get me some coffee and took my favorite book to read and again moved to balcony made me comfortable and had a sip of coffee and started to read a new chapter titled,"Shooting star" this title remembered me about my past life from childhood.

I could remember the full moon day, and my fasting for it. I continued this fasting at every full moon day till my college days and one day I found a shooting star and I started to pray for my need , at schooling I wished to get rank holder and in college to have a good life but every time my motto of life got changed and even my wish.

None of my wish was fulfilled, because I didn't work for it. But my heart didn't recognize that time, and it reflected the anger of mine.

And I came out of my homeland and ran to find my destiny. Life is not a simple thing, but it's a wonderful chance given by almighty to change our live with the choices we get.

I looked back at my path and found my fault, that the only thing I done since in my life is,

I made only wishes, but didn't work for it.

Half life of mine just gone like this, and now I found my real fault, and decided not to just wish for my dreams but to work hard for it.

The evening star always, guided me and now it taught me a good lesson for my life and from this long journey ,I have learnt that every night there may be shooting star,but my wishes cannot be end as last wish.

BELIEVE IN HARDWORK THAN YOUR DREAM,SURE IT WILL TAKE YOU TO THE DREAMS

A.Priyadharshini

She is A.Priyadharshini. She loves writing and writing is her favorite job.she is hailing from coimbatore.

Grey Hair

Growing up just like the speed of light
Along evolution of change with fright
Fills my memories again towards past
On happy frame that shattered so fast
Beside her I driven the heaven filled life
Sculpting me fine with her traditional rife
Made my life colorful since the birth,
Where my presence is only her mirth
Surrounded by pals who lifted me up
And now by thorns that turns me sap
Screaming loud inside with full of stress
Then and now struggling with its mess
Secrets of pain treasured inside my vein
Erupted like a tears hidden in drops of rain
Waiting with all my patience to look again
The days enjoyed with my gray haired shine
My happiness is rare like the fall of comet
That fells with all the flaws from its mate
I wished again and again the one I loved
To make my life filled with loves she carved"

(1)

Life is rare like shooting star ,utilize before it falls

(2)

 Falling is not a new one, but fall like no one with great victory

(3)

 Though there are Infinite stars,people always looks for a fall of star

(4)

Don't panic for a fall

(5)

Shine with all your imperfects and fall with all perfects"

Flairs and Glairs, a platform by a student for the students. We are esteemed youth struggling to carve out our path for our future and we follow a basic mindset Since everyone is not born with all-round skills. Joining hands with people who are born to execute it with perfection is the best way to evolve. Self-Evolution is the need of the hour but, evolving as a community is what we strive for. The initiative as kickstarted by, Founder- Mr. Shubham Shah with the motive to utilize the skillset and talent of writing has now a team of 10+ people who are actively participating into newer forms of learning and discovering talents among youngsters. We Provide platform and services like Publishing opportunities, Open mics, Workshops, Hands-on training. Operating with Brand Name Of Flairs and Glairs (Publication House), we offer the chance of elevating a passionate writer to an esteemed author With Brand name Teekhe Zasbaaat, We bring to you an opportunity to get accustomed with the Public Speaking and Presenting of Thoughts along with regular challenges to brush up your inking spirit. The newest initiative to extend our services we introduced in a new writing Platform- The Glittering Fables and Ink Over Tears.

We Choose to Fly Like A Falcon than to be a

Leg Pulling Crab.

To Know More: Infoline – 7781900870
Mail Us At-
flairsandglairs@gmail.com / info@flairsandglairs.in
Or Visit is at
www.flairsandglairs.com / www.flairsandglairs.in
Social Handles- @flairsandglairs @teekhezasbaaat

www.ingramcontent.com/pod-product-compliance
Lightning Source LLC
LaVergne TN
LVHW050931200726